Fledglings

A collection of poetry
and short stories

Gorey Writers

Boland Press

First published in 2016
Copyright © the authors

Boland Press
Grove Mill
Hollyfort
Co. Wexford
http://bolandpress.blogspot.com

A CIP catalogue record for this book
is available from the British Library

ISBN: 978-1-907855-16-0

Gorey Writers Group gratefully acknowledges
financial assistance from
Wexford County Council

Cover design: Barrett Editing
Cover image: ©Shutterstock.com/Tanor

Printed in Ireland by
SprintPrint

The Gorey Writers
meet fortnightly on a
Thursday evening in
Gorey Library.
Fledglings is the group's
first collection of poetry
and short stories.

Acknowledgement is given to the following publications where some of these poems, or versions of them, have appeared:

Time and Tide, Boland Press
Same Train, Different Track, Boland Press

Gorey Writers wish to thank Gorey Library and Wexford County Council for facilitating Gorey Writers' meetings.

Foreword

It was a Sunday afternoon in late summer when I first encountered the Gorey Writers Group, whose work is sampled in this anthology. We were to meet, I had been told, at the bridge, down the hill from Hollyfort Village. There were going to be poems – and good things to eat. I liked the sound of both.

Carol and Bernie were already waiting in the memorial garden there. It had been opened only recently, a tribute to Máire Comerford and Aileen Keogh, two women of the district who, as members of Cumann na mBan, had cycled from North Wexford to Dublin to play their part in the Easter Rising. We chatted about these courageous ladies until the others had arrived, and then set off, snaking in single file through the trees beside the north bank of the River Bann. Here and there along the path sheets of paper were hanging from branches or pinned to trees. Each one bore a poem. Then we would stop for a moment, while one of the company read the poem aloud. The words sounded through the air above the babbling of the river, before fading and losing themselves among the trees. I remember something by W B Yeats, and 'The Force that through the Green Fuse Drives the Flower', that extraordinary poem written by Dylan

Thomas when he was only nineteen. It made me think of the links that there are between the natural world and the world of poetry.

While she was matron at Mount St. Benedict, Dom. Fr. Sweetman's school outside Gorey, Aileen Keogh collected beautiful roses to grow in the old garden there. The origin of the word 'anthology' lies in the Greek *anthos*, meaning 'flower', and *-logia*, meaning 'collection'. In Greek, the word originally was used for an assembly of the 'flowers' of verse, short, exquisite poems or epigrams by various authors. And so it is pleasing that in this anthology, many of the poems, and some of the prose pieces, are rooted in the natural world – one or two of them, indeed, were written on that memorable day by the river at Hollyfort.

The poems here vary widely in tone and subject, but they share a vividness of expression that is not always found in writing today. Full of colour, they show the fruits of *really looking.* Again and again, the reader is forced to pause over a phrase or an image that is as fresh as a spring day: 'pools of sky blue eyes', or 'sunlight beams through woods', or the 'ginger and snow-white perfection' of a cat, or in Carol Boland's 'The Buzzard', 'summer breeze holding her / in open play above the tillage field'.

And it is appropriate that the title of this anthology, *Fledglings*, itself comes from nature.

Fledglings are, as we know, young birds that have recently grown their feathers, but have not yet learned to fly. Some of the writers in these pages may be quite new to writing, but it would be unfair to conclude that their words cannot take flight. And it is not only in the poems. The ten prose pieces published here contain much that is striking and thought-provoking: the memory of a day on the beach near Arklow, to take a random example from many, is beautifully told, and – though no great events or emotional traumas are involved – the effect on the reader is unexpectedly moving. It may be something to do with the exact recreation in words of sensations and details – how it feels to push a heavy pram through soft sand, or to experience the now forgotten delight of soggy tomato and salad cream sandwiches. Elsewhere, we read of an incident during the War of Independence which might have ended in tragedy, but didn't: the tale is told so economically that it seems to have been projected into the reader's mind like a photograph on a screen. But enough – you will discover many more such treasures in these pages yourself.

In his poem 'In the (p)ink', Chris Black speaks of doing 'a little word knitting'. He is being too modest: the writing in *Fledglings* amounts to much more than a craft or a pastime. Each of us will understand and appreciate the poems and stories here in our own individual way. That is what makes any collection such as this so exciting. For, as we read, the words on the page will open a direct link between the writer's mind and our own. It is a link that may be impossible to forge in any other way – something quite different and more intimate than, say, two people having a chat. The direct communication that arises, through the medium of a book, from carefully chosen words flowing freely from one mind into another, may in fact be closer to love.

John Wyse Jackson

Be like the bird, who
halting in his flight
on limb too slight
feels it give way beneath him
yet sings
knowing he hath wings.

Victor Hugo

CONTENTS

Fledglings

Bernie Walsh is a family historian. She founded Gorey Writers in 2006 and enjoys writing short stories. Recently, she has ventured into poetry.

Passing time

She just sits there
in her easy chair
remote for up, remote for down,
recline, incline, resign
to no more walking into town.

Blankly staring at the wall
waiting for someone to call
maybe her son, his trophy wife
2.4 children with their fancy life.

Recline, incline, resign
to meals on wheels,
veg soup
creamed rice
steak and kidney pud.

She just sits there
in her easy chair
remote for up, remote for down
recline, incline, resign
to passing time.

Bernie Walsh

The Canvas

He painted her in red
reflecting pools of sky blue eyes
soft skin of palest white
fingers long and tender.

He sang to her of
love, lust and being
always there
beside her all the way.

She was his scarlet lady,
lost his way in her shallowness
but everything has a price
only a brush stroke on a canvas.

Bernie Walsh

The Women of 1916

She cleans and cooks
feeds the men
rides her bike
sneaks into town
to put political posters
on blank walls
collects the bullets
for the guns
nurses the soldiers
shot in brawls
washes the bodies
brings in the coal
stays up all night
to darn socks and sew
by a small fire, just a glow
a woman of 1916 on the go
100 years on
what changes.

Chris Black, writer and poet from Wexford, has been writing for over 20 years. His first book, *Same Train, Different Track,* was published in 2016.

In the (p)ink

Sitting here quite content
with my brand new writing implement
what could be more fitting than to do
a little word knitting?
Unravel the contents of the alphabet
and see how further on I get
this is not a challenge or a work against my will,
be patient be still
discount pressure as though it did not exist
write a poem with a twist
a poem with a double rhyme which will
accommodate each line
something different for a change
it really will not be that strange
sitting here quite content this will be time
well spent.

My brand new writing implement will never be a
substitute for my quill
but just indeed to have a choice to give this
fountain pen a voice is indeed a challenge
not to be cast aside this is fact I tell you
not to be denied.

If this present was not received think on this,
this poem would not have been conceived so for
me it is a joyous occasion to sit and witness this
word explosion
breathing new life as it were into this poem
with loving care.
A brand new piece one of a kind, rough
around the edges not quite refined
it will grow I have no doubt, hope someone
will embrace,
this task will then be done and
it will have run its race
sitting here in quite contentment,
thank you for the present,
money well spent.

The Old Timer

He stood leaning across the wooden fencing drinking in the bright multi-colours of a field in full bloom. A field festooned with wild flowers, purple, red and orange, in fact all colours of the rainbow and then some.

Years of hard graft and now a comfort in old age, flowers were his passion, whether growing wild or in his hothouses. People came from far and near to purchase shrubs, potted plants, flowers to adorn graves, wedding bouquets, and blooms for all occasions. Return visitors year-on-year placed orders for ceremonies in graveyards throughout the county and bordering counties. His personality was an attraction as much as his flowers.

Living alone and ageing, the business was becoming not so much a burden as a hobby. As well as earning him a good living, it gave him something to get up for each breaking dawn. The arthritis, now that was a problem. His hands were beginning to stiffen up with all the bending and stooping and this was playing on his mind. He was also becoming more forgetful day by day, which was frustrating. Leave something out of his hand, he'd spend half an hour looking for it, only to find he planted it earlier.

It was getting close to decision time. No one could make the decision for him. People could give him all the advice they wanted but, at the end of the day, he had to make the final choice. So there he was leaning across this wooden fence pondering his life or what there was left of it. What should he do? Where would he go? One sure fact, he could not stay around and see the business bought and then razed to the ground. Or watch people come and go on a daily basis, purchasing *his* flowers as though nothing had changed.

House and property went on the market as a single lot. A chapter of his life was closed. The thought of it was breaking his heart. What had he to look forward to? A future without flower gardens to tend was not something he ever anticipated; now it was quickly becoming a reality. Feeling tired and emotional, he retired for one last night in his home.

They placed a wreath of flowers from his beloved gardens on his grave, two days after the sale.

Carol Boland is a performance poet and Poetry Therapy Practitioner. Her published books include *The Overture* and *Hostage.*

The Coupling

She carries him
     in the folds of her dress
     crease of her elbow
     smile of her hips
or knotted fast in the roots
of her jet hair
like a child's comb.

He carries her
     in the blue of his jeans
     the furrow of his brow
     pride of his shoulders
or bedded in his lyrics
on white sheets
strewn across the day.

These women knew their place
for Aileen and Máire

We plant a garden
on cleared, re-seeded ground
to remember new beginnings
look towards the hills of Hollyfort
where hope dared to dream
in the tobacco fields and ditches.

We plant three granite stones
for remembrance
a path to lead the way
a flag to fly
in the face of despair.

These women nursed their visions
never faltered in the chase
for in the story of this land
these women knew their place.

Carol Boland

The Buzzard

I spy her on my morning walk
a shadow in the drizzle
summer breeze holding her
in open play above the tillage field
wings stationary
brown against the grey
eyes eagle-like
radar red.

I lean my breath on gun-metal bars
splattered with dung
eyes strained
ears attune to soaring silence.

Morning hunger drags me downhill
under drenched trees
until halted in my tracks
a bandit of crows attempt
to cut-up the copious wings
to fell her like a giant redwood
release the dangling rabbit from her claws.

Grace O'Reilly hails from Bray and now lives in Gorey, Co. Wexford. Published in several magazines, including *Irish Parent Magazine*, she is now working on a novel.

Goodbye
i.m. Grandmother Eileen Power

I feel you on a breezy day
I feel your love through a sunny ray
I feel you in the wind and rain
I feel your love beneath the pain.

Memories of sleepovers and of fun times
of playing scrabble, cards and of lullabies
I believe you are in heaven looking down
I close my eyes and you are all around.

Today was hard with our final goodbye
yet I know I'll see you in a butterfly
hear you in a song or poem
know I'll never be alone.

Weigh to Go

I have always had issues and insecurities about my weight. Maybe that's just me being a typical woman living in a modern world, or maybe that is just me. Or maybe it is because I was bullied at school. All I know is that I have never been happy with the way that I look.

Last year I was at my heaviest ever at 13 stone 3 lbs. Now, 9 months on, I am 10 stone 7 lbs. I still have a way to go until I reach my target weight, yet have lost more than I planned to lose at this stage; mentally, I have gained so much more.

In October 2013, I rang Anne Dixon from Unislim in distress. I was literally on the last leg of being miserable about my weight. I ripped the whole ass out of a brand new pair of trousers my mother had bought me and was so ashamed. I had only got them over the top of my legs when I heard the sound of material ripping: my heart broke too. It was a blessing though, because the new lease of life that Ann, Jan and all the members in Unislim, as well as my friends and family, have given me is unreal.

After I had my two children I dreaded shopping. I liked the idea of food shopping and tossing crap like chocolate in the basket to gorge on later: the truth of it is that it didn't make me feel good, just worse. As Anne said last

Christmas, dressed with a turkey hat on her head, 'If you gobble, gobble, gobble you will wobble, wobble, wobble. But if you nibble, nibble, nibble you can jiggle, jiggle, jiggle'. It is true, when I dress up now I feel sexy and confident. My husband Simon always told me I was beautiful and he loved me. But I never loved me and that was the problem.

I can look in the mirror now and not cry. I can get up in the morning and choose to dress in style with use of my trusty *U Magazine*. Or simply stay in my pjs because I am having a lazy day with fun and movies with Olivia and Ben, our three and one-year-old. Not because I can't be bothered getting dressed and going outside because, God forbid, I may scare the kitty cat next door!

Now I dress up and feel good. I am not vain by any stretch, but am just becoming more satisfied and accepting of who I am. I enjoy getting my hair done and buying smaller clothes. It makes me feel good inside and out. I have more energy, more get up and go. Apart from me and my husband, it is great for my two youngsters that I can play and keep up with them, especially now the little man is on the move. I drive now too.

Yes, I know it is not Christmas yet, but Anne gave us a picture of a Christmas tree. Every time we lose weight we colour in a bauble, though are not allowed to touch the star until Christmas week when we can all shine together. I hope to reach my target weight by then, and not only will my Christmas tree light up but so will I.

Aoife Barrett was inspired to
start writing again after moving
to Poulshone, Co. Wexford in
2015. She is now working on
a crime novel.

Piano Concerto in A Major

To the right of the orchestra, silent
the grand piano shines in spotlight.
A winged lid showing strings, pliant.
The audience in an expectant hush.

She arrives, stellar in a red velvet dress,
polite applause in greeting as she disposes.
There is no sense of any strain or stress,
a virtuoso's smile, as the first note sounds.

Maestro's baton a blur, hands in motion.
Thousands of sixty minutes practising, all for this:
one moment, one touch, an alchemist's potion,
magical symbiosis – Mozart, her and us.

The elephant tusk keys bring a sense of the dead
as her hands fly over their ebony counterparts.
An invisible metronome ticks in her head,
notes flowing, building to the crescendo.

Reality Check

Alison almost fell out of the car, catching her foot
on the safety belt. So embarrassing. She hitched
her Marc Jacob sunglasses back into place and
acted nonchalant as she opened the petrol cap
and started filling up her dad's BMW. He'd only
lent it to her on the strict understanding that she
returned it with a full tank. He was beyond cheap
– closer to miser level. He'd even refused to buy
her the latest Orla Kiely handbag – she'd
explained it wasn't like she was asking for a
Chanel or something, but he'd just like pretended
he didn't get the point. So mean.

She started inching towards €40 on the clock.
As far as she was concerned that was full enough
for the old skinflint. She got it bang on the dial
and carefully placed the nozzle back in its slot.
The last thing she wanted was petrol drops on her
Louboutins.

Clicking the auto-locking, Alison sauntered
towards the shop to settle up.
'Would you have any spare change, Miss?'
'Oh . . . , eh . . . no, sorry,' she muttered,
accelerating into the shop. She'd half-noticed him,
but just thought he was waiting for someone.
Yeah, he looked a bit thin and 70s-throwback in
his matching denim jacket and jeans; she'd
clocked that in a peripheral way. Why did these
guys have to turn up in the weirdest places and

ambush people at like 10am on a Sunday morning? A petrol station on the motorway wasn't the best plan either. It was fairly deserted at this hour.

Hiding behind the coffee machine as she grabbed a skinny decaf cappuccino to go, she had a closer recce. He looked about 40, pretty worn out with lank brown-blond hair, a sad goatee and faded blue eyes. He was a good height, same as her brother Dylan so around 6 feet, but talk about fragile looking. Maybe she should have just given him a few euro? His life must be pretty desperate if this was his great plan on how to make a living. Then again, it'd be like her dad was always saying and she'd just be encouraging the guy to stay there begging all day. The miser, of course, didn't give out any hand-outs. He donated through his company, getting some kind of big kickback on tax relief, and thought he was Mother Teresa. He'd given her a lecture about it the last time he caught her slipping €5 to a woman who was begging on Grafton Street. Luckily her mum was there for that one and had cut across all his bluster:

'She has a dog, David; surely you can't blame Alison for wanting to make sure the poor dog doesn't starve?' Her mum was the only one who could ever get her dad to shut up and see reason.

Alison forced the lid down on the cardboard cup, narrowly avoiding getting third degree burns. She was wondering if she should just buy the guy a coffee – well, not a skinny version obviously, as it didn't look like he had to worry about all those extra pounds; the guy didn't know how lucky he was in some ways. She could get him like an americano or maybe a latte but then he might prefer tea and a muffin. They'd a good deal going, both for €4. No it'd be better to just give him money so he could like buy whatever he wanted himself.

She saw a woman walking past the guy, shaking her head no and barking something. She looked really angry but it was weird the beggar's expression never changed. He looked totally blank. It was a bit scary.

Alison kept her eye on him as she headed for the pay desk. Maybe it'd be better if she just pretended she was on a call on her way out. All she had to do was press her iPhone to her ear and who was to know? Yeah, that was a better plan. She didn't want to give him some money now and then always be running into him here. Talk about awkward. No, her dad was right. She wouldn't give the guy anything. She'd just ignore him and go home and donate to some proper homeless charity instead.

'That's €3 for the cappuccino; any petrol or diesel?' the Asian assistant asked, sounding totally bored. There was no point saying anything to her about the guy. She was so obviously giving the minimum wage effort to her job. They'd like have to pay her danger money to confront a beggar at the shop's door.

'Yes, €40 on number eh . . . just over there . . . the black BMW.'

'Number 5, right?'

'Yeah . . . ok,' Alison said, handing over €50.
'And that's €7 change.'
'Thanks.'

Alison grabbed the money and headed for the door. If she timed this right she wouldn't even need her mobile. She'd be going through the door just as the guy who'd jumped out of the white van was coming in. He was strutting across the forecourt, 5ft 2ins of cocky male, all muscle and looking fit enough to do an ironman challenge. She knew the type, full of small man syndrome. He was like an economics lecturer she'd had in college who thought he was God's gift.

She reached for the door just in time to hear: 'Excuse me, do you have any spare change?' God's gift gave the beggar one scornful look and smiled aggressively.

'Yeah I've got change mate . . . loads of it. Why don't you get a fuckin job instead of standing there all day annoying people? Then you'd have some yourself.'

He breezed into the shop as Alison came out stifling an embarrassed laugh. She gave the beggar a quick sidelong glance not wanting to make eye contact. Talk about mortifying. But his expression hadn't changed at all. He looked straight through her and asked: 'Would you have any spare change, Miss?'

Carmel Conroy is a recent member of the group. She writes for pleasure and particularly enjoys writing short stories.

Nurse Glover

Cathedral Close nestled in the shadow of the Cathedral of the Assumption. A quiet cul de sac, it contained twelve houses and was lined with sycamore trees on either side.

She lived two doors away from our house. Although many years retired, she was always given her full title of Nurse Glover. Small of stature, with steel grey hair, she walked with the air of one much taller. She came from what was described at the time as 'good stock'. Winter or summer, she never left the house without her purple felt hat held securely in place with a pearl hatpin. A stickler for punctuality, she walked the short lane to church before the bells had a chance to announce it was time for Mass. I thought she was a hundred years old but found out later from her headstone that she was, in fact, seventy-two.

On that first morning I had to kneel on a chair in her front room window to see out. I was hoping to spot my siblings pass by on their way to school. It had snowed overnight. Every bare branch on the trees outside was defined, and the snow lay like soapflakes on the ground.

Everything was new and unfamiliar. The room served as kitchen-cum-dining room. A great big fire was lit in a black cast iron fireplace in which pine logs were hissing and spitting in contrast to the otherwise silent room. Two Dresden china ladies sat on either side of a brown clock on the mantelpiece. A couch was placed near the fire with a book sitting on the arm rest. The couch was covered with a multi-coloured crochet rug. At the far end of the room she was busy taking cups and saucers from a pine dresser. And so began a new chapter for the next nine months. Every morning just before 9 a.m. I was welcomed into her home. My father had died a few weeks previously and my mother was left to care for three small children. In order to provide for us, she had no choice but to return to work. I was only three and not of school going age like my siblings. Nurse Glover had offered to take care of me during the working hours.

At precisely 10 a.m. each morning, tea was taken. A tray covered with a white cloth was carried to the table. On it were two china cups and saucers. These were yellow and painted with delicate blue cornflowers. Kneeling on my chair at the table, I waited as she buttered wafer-thin brown bread. This was then covered with delicious orange 'jam' which was spooned from a pot with a picture of a black cat sleeping at a fire. I had never tasted anything like it – especially the orange chewy bits. I still think fondly of her when I see 'Fruitfield Old Time Irish Marmalade'.

After tea was taken, she liked to read. I would sometimes remain at the table with my colouring books and crayons, or sit on the rug near the fire playing with my doll Yum-yum. At other times I would wander into her good room or parlour, as she like to call it. A glass cabinet stood regally in the corner. This contained a collection of dolls from around the world. Many an hour was spent in an imaginary world where only a three-year-old can go.

Thursday was library day. Hand-in-hand we would walk the short distance to Dublin Street to return books and stock up on reading material for the next seven days. The library was housed in a very old building and it would be impossible to forget the smell of books old and new, which is unique to libraries even today. After what seemed like hours – picking up and putting down, reading and re-reading front and back covers – books were finally chosen. Although unable to read at the time, and too young to join, I was allowed to choose a book from the junior section and add it to her selection. On one of these occasions a book cover with a picture of a little boy sitting in a shiny red car took my fancy. And so began my love of Noddy books. It was also the beginning of my passion for reading. The books were carried to the front desk. Miss McCloud, the librarian, would then stamp the little cards and replace them in the little pickets stuck inside each book. They were then placed in our wicker shopping basket, ready for the journey home.

A detour to Mrs Kelly's sweet shop on the corner was a must. A little bell inside the door would tinkle to announce our arrival. Behind the dark wooden counter, the shelves groaned beneath the various glass jars of bull's-eyes, bonbons, clove drops and sweets every colour of the rainbow. I would eagerly wait for Mrs Kelly to hand over acid drops for Nurse Glover, and a sherbet dip dab for myself. I adored the fizzy feeling on my tongue and the way it would always make its way up my nose making it tickle. Every last grain would be devoured with the help of the lollies supplied. This would then be licked until it too disappeared.

September came around all too quickly. It was time for me to start school. Every evening as we passed her house on the way home, the front curtain would twitch. That was my invitation to run in and say 'hello'.

One wet November evening, on my way home from school, I noticed that her curtain remained still. With the help of neighbours, we found that my friend and mentor was ill. She was taken to hospital where she spent her last remaining weeks. On one of our visits she placed a little blue velvet box in my hand. It contained her nurse's fob watch. Although no longer working now, it still takes pride of place on my dressing table.

Most of us, if fortunate enough, encounter at least one person that leaves an indelible mark on our journey through life. Such was my experience with this special lady. As she sits in her eternal armchair, I sincerely hope and pray that the good Lord above keeps her well supplied with romantic novels, acid drops and, of course, 'Fruitfield Old Time Irish Marmalade'.

Veronica Lombard is a member
of Gorey Little Theatre. She enjoys
the writers' sessions with the
writers' group in Gorey Library.

The Carnival

The carnival came to town every year
carousels, bumpers, chairoplanes, rifle range,
hoops, stalls with statues, pictures,
delph, vases, beautiful dolls
under a kaleidoscope of coloured bulbs
last few tickets, roll up, roll up.
Hearts thumped wildly as the wheel spun
round and round
number 24, yes here.
Ring the gold fish bowl and bring it home,
Ah ha! Nearly did it, one more go.
Anyone else for the swinging boats?

Pulling my father's hand I urge him on.
Big strong hands lift me into the boat
then, in a second my dad sitting opposite me
away, away, away, we fly up and down
who cares if he's the oldest swinger in town.

Veronica Lombard

Pamela

Memories fill my mind
and you, old friend,

you and your wonderful imagination
that filled the rest of us with awe.

Elvis, Bob Dylan on your record player
played slowly so we could write the words.

Your blue Volkswagen that travelled us far
the stopping because you had weak kidneys.

The Spanish holiday where romance blossomed
Arnaldo and you, me and your man.

You, icing our Christmas cake with squiggles
and pump tops of all shapes and sizes.

The stylish outfits worn with panache
dainty hands with painted nails.

You, picked to dance in the front row
Carousel, Oklahoma, The Boyfriend.

The thumbing to Kerry on our first holiday
Pairc Bui, the Caravan, the dances, the lads,

you smoking Peter Stuyvesant elegantly.
Baby Cham, Sherry, Bacardi and Coke.

The parting when I married. Distancing us.
Change as our roads diverged.

Last weekend you passed away.
What ifs? Why? It was as you wished.

Private and oh, so quiet
Molly your dog to be with you.

Go forth, dear Pamela,
may the rain fall gently on your resting place.

Veronica Lombard

Niamh Cinn Oir

She had such a little life.
I told her this was her place
where she would live and laugh
and have her being.

The start was beautiful
the first child of deep love
the first child of us
the first child of family.
How could it be that we were faced
with recessive gene
that would take her little life
that would be one in four in future
that would nail us silent.

What if our Niamh Cinn Oir is, as
my sister said, in the arms of my mother.
The fortune teller said.
I can imagine my beloved mother
will hold her until I arrive
and take her to my heart again.

Mary Keogh Hansen is from
Arklow and has a keen interest
in crime writing. She is working
on her autobiography which she
hopes to publish.

Memories are made of this

Growing up in Arklow on the east coast of Ireland
was a blessing. The beach where we spent our
childhood summers was one of those godsends.

The walk to either of the two beaches was a
long one from our council house. It didn't seem to
bother us then, myself and six siblings. The
journey would take us down through the ditch.
This was dotted all the way along with blackberry
bushes. In autumn, armed with our tin cans, we
would pick and devour the berries, our mouths
and hands stained purple from the juice. Some of
them still made their way into the tin cans and
Mammy would then create exquisite jam and
tarts. On either side of the bushes were luscious
green fields with cows chewing their cud, lazing in
the summer sun.

Of course, there was the usual tipping and
tapping of one another along the way. Poor
Mammy would have to intervene a few times
before we reached the beach.

The North and South beaches were linked by
a bridge, 'The Nineteen Arches' under which the

Avoca River flows. We usually opted to go to the North side which took us over the bridge. Even on the warmest summer day there was always a sea breeze carrying the scent of saltiness. The excitement among us was palpable. The smaller ones would latch onto the big Silver Cross pram that not only housed the baby but towels, swimsuits, buckets and spades, food, flask of tea and blankets.

Finally we arrived. We all lent a hand in pulling the pram up the sandy hill into the dunes. This was a bit of a struggle as the sand was fine-grained and the wheels of the pram would submerge, but it was worth the effort. The dunes with their tall spiked grasses formed a barrier from the sea breeze on a windy day.

First thing to go were our sandals, our little feet would start doing a jig as they touched the hot glistening sand. The contents of the pram including the baby were taken out. The blankets would be spread over the warm sand and my baby brother put sitting on it. Then the race to grab the few towels we had to share. We would put these around us to hide our bits and pieces while we dropped our underwear to the ground, with one hand still holding onto the towel while trying to jiggle into our togs. Then a dart to the shoreline with our buckets and spades, skipping gingerly over the sharp stones and shells.

My two older brothers could swim but we were content to sit at the water's edge splashing each other, letting the icy cold water rush over our bodies. We created castles and dams from the damp slightly stony sand at the shore, gathering bigger stones and shells to make walls. Often we would take it in turns to bury each other up to the neck and see if we could mobilise ourselves from the sand grave.

Around about the same time as our stomachs would start to rumble, Mammy would call out to us to come get food. That morning she would have buttered what seemed to us mountains of bread to make sandwiches. There was the usual Calvita and Galtee cheese ones, some with tomatoes and salad cream, which were a bit soggy by the time we got to eat them. However, hunger is a good sauce and we munched them down with gusto. As a special treat, we would wash them down with Cream or Lemon Soda lemonade. We all had plastic cups but Mammy had a tin cup that she drank her tea from.

We sat in the dunes chattering, laughing, fighting. So many contrasting sounds: grasshoppers making clicking noises, seagulls squawking, waiting for any crumbs that might fall from our laps. When sated, we lay down to dry ourselves off in our togs. The feelings of cosiness and warmth, snuggled in the dunes with our wet togs, drying on our bodies underneath the blue sky, are quite vivid even now.

Mammy would try to rub off any grains of sand from our bodies with a towel which could sting at times because of sunburn. Suntan lotion was expensive in those days and the bad effects

of overexposure to sun was not as well known
then as it is now.

It was time to do the reverse of what we had
started, putting back on our clothes with as little
exposure of our skins as possible. We were very
modest then. The pram was loaded up. Even
though we were tired now, it was easier pulling it
down out of the dunes. Off we set on our journey
back to our small house.

There was very little bickering on the way
back as our energy had been spent on the beach.
We had beetroot but happy heads as we made
our way home. The journey seemed to take
longer, possibly due to the fact that we were
jaded but relaxed from all the activity and, of
course, from inhaling the sea air. When home, we
had to be individually hosed down in the bath to
get rid of any residue of sand. Then our faces
and limbs would be spread with Calamine lotion
which made us look like peculiar pink ghosts.

Sadly, the dunes no longer exist. The North
Beach is practically non-existent due to necessary
protection works. However, you can still enjoy the
scent and view of the sea from the lovely board-
walk which runs the full length of what used to be
our playground in summer.

Myles Carroll is a recent member of Gorey Writers. He has a great interest in nature and enjoys writing and telling stories.

Wildflower Garden

It is that time again
when all seems lost and gone away
it is so lonely here right now
and nothing seems like yesterday
when all your heads just tossed and swayed
and played a part in nature's way.
You brought together many varied friends
some were crawling and more flying in
but being here was their intent.

For me right now
I must revive and look myself
to lift my sights and start again
and if, however, you cannot make it back
you will be remembered like all the rest
for the shine and brightness that you gave
to the Wildflower Garden.

Eggs-it

Now, I'm going to tell you a story about myself but I am going to ask you one favour: don't tell anyone about this, not even the person sitting beside you, and don't tell Therese, my wife, if she is down there listening. She is not to know about these things.

Anyway, during the course of my working life, I happened to be Branch Secretary of Arklow and Gorey Offices and, on occasions, I had to travel over to Gorey to discuss issues with the Branch Manager whose name was Barry. I remember one particular Friday afternoon I was over in his office and during our discussions a postman knocked on the door, entered the room and left a half dozen of eggs on Barry's table. Being of an impetuous nature myself, I thought the eggs might come in handy if things go wrong.

Anyway, we continued on and at the end of our conversation Barry said to me 'Do you want to take home the eggs?' I said that they were given to him. 'Well', he said, 'would you not take half of them?' I said fair enough. He said he had nothing to put them in and I said don't worry I'll be careful with them. So, I put two in one pocket and one in the other, said goodbye and thanked him.

I was now out on the Avenue walking along with my two hands down in my pockets holding on to my eggs. I had turned the corner and was heading down the top of the town. I had the car parked below in Pettitt's carpark. Everything was going lovely and then, out of the corner of my eye, I saw this lady crossing the street. Oh God, she was a real stunner. And do you know what happened me? I lost control of my eggs and walked straight into a telegraph pole, bursting up two eggs in my pocket.

Oh, Holy God, I was in an awful state. There was egg here, there and everywhere. I was so embarrassed I thought I'd never make it back to the car. I could not go shopping or anything, only go straight home.

When I got home, my wife saw the state I was in. I tried to tell her about getting the eggs and clipping off a pole coming down the street. She said to me: Are you blind? Can you not see where you are going? Or what do you be thinking about?

Between all the questioning and giving out, I never got a chance to tell her about the young lady crossing the street.

The River
An Acrostic Poem

The high shining moon
Hangs brightly
Enhancing the
Rippling water
Inviting me towards
Verge of
Ever flowing
River.

Jazz Stynes joined the writers' group in 2015 and loves the poetry, especially Haiku, and short stories. She finds meetings inspiring but all too short.

Six Haiku

A green fern unfurls
up from the damp woodland floor
forty shades of green.

Wild garlic bluebells
soft spongy earth green trees
sunlight beams through woods.

Round bales wrapped in green
gold straw stacked like cubes toasting
old stone church – silence.

Peacocks, admirals
snow white buddleia blossoms
leaves turning to red.

The last red rose blooms
before the harsh autumn wind
whips her velvet coat.

Feet crunch autumn leaves
as children play trick or treat
red noses – silver stars.

Census Woman

It was the census advertisement on the television
that brought it all back to my mind, my job as a
census enumerator in West Cork. I was so
obedient, no other person in the car, do not forget
your forms '*as Gaeilge*,' vital and strictly
confidential information held close to my chest,
even to this very day. Marking each house
carefully on the map every night having arrived
home exhausted after a long day trekking.
Nobody warned you about the mad dogs at the
farm gates who nipped your tyres and size eleven
wellington boots.

I arrived in the valley, surrounded by huge
rocks, it was like Indian Territory, just out of an
American western movie. Smoke rising from
cottages and me with a heavy briefcase over my
shoulder, armed with forms, a pair of wellingtons
from the husband, wearing ten pairs of socks to
keep them on, and a big Aran cardigan. I set out
for my most important task.

The farms were a good bit apart, so I had to
use the car to get me to a certain point then hike
over the lanes to the cottages. I proceeded down
one long lane, avoiding potholes full of water, and
spotted a responsible looking man leaning on a
big shovel, watching me from under the rimless
glasses, eyes peeled with a look of wonder on his
face as to who was this woman coming down the

lane. 'Good morning,' I said in my friendly voice. 'I am the census woman.'

'Right so,' he replied, 'you better come in then. Where are you from, girl?' he quizzed me on the short walk to the house.

'Oh, Meath' I replied. 'Only here a couple of months.'

'What's a Meath woman here doing our census,' he quizzed again.

'Well sure it was advertised in the paper, you could have applied yourself,' I said back.

Well, his hearty laugh echoed up the lane and down the valley. 'Come in, come in, sure you just missed my friend the bishop, and if he has left any of the lovely pavlova, you can have a taste.'

I walked through the sunny glass porch and stopped, open mouthed, to look at the most beautiful geraniums in all kinds of containers all lined up like soldiers on the window sills. All in great condition, all the same height and in full blossom. As the man entered the door he shouted out 'Peadar, the census lady is here,' to his brother. They both fussed over me, set the table, cut up the pavlova and put it on the best china plate with the cream flowing over the side. Fresh tea made in the china pot, drank from the best china tea cup.

'Now, I hope you have brought me an Irish form, girl,' the man said, who I now knew as Padraig.

'Yes, I have,' I said as I handed over the form. Mission accomplished, I headed off up the lane to the next house.

I was greeted immediately with 'Ah, there you are, I knew you were coming,' said a lady standing in her apron, her hands looked like she was in the middle of baking. She must have seen smoke signals or an arrow head that had shot across the valley, as there were no mobile phones in them days. Lovely people, all curious to know about me, and my life since I moved to the area.

Eventually, I got to the end of the lane, bursting at the seams with tea and cake. One more house and then I'd be on my way home. It was a quiet cottage, the front door wide open. I walked in to darkness at the front door, like the black hole of Calcutta.

'Hello, hello, is there anybody home,' I shouted, not wanting to frighten any occupants.

'Come in, come in,' said a voice from the darkness. I stopped inside the door to adjust my eyes and see who belonged to the voice. It took me a while but then I saw him, a smiling, kind little man cutting a slice of bread from a loaf with what I can only describe as a sword, sawing through the loaf as he held it up to his neck like a fiddle. I was imagining him beheading himself when finally the slice broke off. He plastered it with butter and then to my amazement turned and fed it to his donkey. Through the smoke I had not noticed the small donkey standing in the corner.

'There you go, a lovely bit of bread for you too,' he said to his sheepdog. What a triangle of love I witnessed that day between this old man and his animals. I gave him his forms and I trundled up the lane.

The sight of Bantry bay on my left made my heart miss a beat; it was so scenic and calm.

I was just about to hop into the car when, 'Hey, Miss,' a young girl shouted to me. 'You forgot one house. Behind that rock, Miss.' I walked up the steps cut into the rock and there it sat below, I had never seen it. There in the garden, digging, was an elderly lady.

'Sure you'll have a cup of tea with me. You don't mind the top of the milk now girl, do you,' she said pushing a cup towards me.

'Donal is in the bed, not too well at the moment,' she said, pointing to a little door at the corner of the fireplace. She sat down and picked up a large patchwork quilt and started to sew.

Two hours later, I left the lonely woman sewing. I continued on up hills, down boreens, over rocks, under hedges, checking every house and derelict to be counted if they had a roof. I met hippies with gorgeous happy children, Hari Krishnas, Germans, Dutch, and English, all who had made this valley their home. I went from tea and soda bread to being offered red or white wine, that special time I was a census woman.

Catherine MacPartlin joined Gorey Writers following the death of her brother Paul in 9/9/2014. These poems are dedicated to his life and memory. Joining the group and writing has been a very positive and enriching experience for her.

Kitchen Table

People are dying to look like this he said,
he stood erect, chest out
in a 'taa-daa' sort of way!

His audience laughed
sitting around the kitchen table
he, standing on a chair
with that quiet smile of his,
they, laughter fading to rueful smiles,
'Jasus, you're gas.'

He only had 6 months.

Catherine MacPartlin

Going with the flow

You liked that
going with the flow
living your life, facing your death
going with the flow.

I see you by the stream, squatting, reaching in,
fistfuls of pebbles, plop, plop, plopping,
droplets sparkling as they reach to the sky
giddy laughter filling the crisp, clear air

running like a river, finding its way,
through forests of tall, strong trees
gliding through fields of long, silky grass
lazing in the summer sun.

I see you now running stronger
racing through fresh, lush fields
making your way, shaping your own course
windmills tilting to your flow.

With your energy waning, you look to the sea
surrounded by ripened fruit and leafy trees
tender thoughts and loving hearts
going with the flow
you've reached life's ocean.

Polly Chapman is local to
Gorey and new to the group.
Writing for some time, she is
also an avid reader who enjoys
the literary life.

Fledgling

You are leaving me now
roots so established deep
into formidable earth
branches extending upwards
outwards, so keen to embrace
it all, here now, this very second.

I sheltered you from the winds, the rains,
the storms, when you were but a sapling.
Giving anchorage to your youth, innocence
and trusting of every mortal thing.

You are leaving me now
and I am giving you up to the Sun,
the Moon, the Stars, the Earth
knowing that they will protect you on your
journey through this earthly life, and after.

Be well my precious one
nurture your roots with empathy, love for
all living beings,
allow your branches to grow in whatever
direction they will.

And when the storms of life are threatening,
you may weaken and bend
try to remember me
for my roots will always be your anchor.

Emer Barrett is new to Gorey and the writers' group and is finding her feet as a writer.

School Tour

His name is Nick Ganley. He turned ten in April. He stopped talking in April. His father died in April. April was not a good month for Nick Ganley. By June he was failing at school and failing at friendship, just failing. He doesn't think his mum has noticed. She is barely there anymore. Even when she stands right in front of him, her eyes look through him. She's fitting into her thin jeans all the time now but she's not happy about it.

He looks just like his dad, people say, and Gran has explained that looking just like his dad is a great thing but just at the moment it made it hard for his mum to look at him. Just for a little while whenever she looked at Nick she saw his dad and that made her sad but she didn't want Nick to be upset so she was holding herself tightly together and that was making her a little bit like a robot, just at the moment. This is what Gran said and Nick wanted to believe it and did believe it, but in his own head wondered what they all thought he saw when he looked in the mirror. How was the son of a robot meant to behave? Nick couldn't figure it out and stopped talking so he wouldn't make any mistakes while he was trying to make sense of it all.

Now Nick is on the rented coach, on the school tour. Gran was there when the notice fell out of his bag. Gran is there a lot now. She burbled on about how lovely it was that he was getting the opportunity to see a bit of Ireland. She ran down while holding the permission slip and then nodded her head very decisively, fetched a pen and some notes from her handbag and quickly signed the permission slip and stuffed it and the money into the envelope. 'There now, that's done. See you hand that over first thing to your teacher, luvvie.'

So, of course, he opened it first and Gran had signed Mum's name, a really bad fake signature actually. But the curiosity that had flickered over his Gran's weird attitude died out. School, tour, none of it mattered really.

Nick rested his head against the cold glass. The vibrations of the wheels as they poured over the motorway knocked his forehead repetitively against the hard pane. Could he give himself a concussion he wondered but decided to spend all his tiny energy on forcing his skin into the glass. He is concentrating everything he has on keeping his head glued to the window. Ignored by old friends as he has been ignoring them for months.

Overhearing snippets from the teachers, he's in the unpopular seat just behind them, no competition for this seat and no possibility of a seat mate. He has spent months picking up pieces from adults around him. His father died. There was no funeral and none of his relatives have died so he doesn't know what should have happened but from what he gathered from listening in, it wasn't usual for nothing at all to happen. His dad was just gone. Lost at sea, no remains. Then Mum emptied all of Dad's stuff out of the house nearly immediately, so that Nick wondered, did he need to be gone too? Burnt in a pyre - like gypsies did with caravans of the dead, the house feeling as empty as he did inside.

The class trip is to somewhere that recalls bits and pieces of his happy family life to him and life without a dad, a great house with a garden; Nick is vaguely aware that he would have probably enjoyed it – before. He wanders on his own mostly and it doesn't even register that the teachers keep a worried eye on him. He has become incalculable and unexpected. Dangerous traits in a child, especially on a school trip. In the staff room his name has been mentioned. 'He'll be fine,' is the general chorus. A kid not being 'fine' with grief is not a path any of the professionals want to tread.

On the way home they pull off the motorway in some small town for a short break. Most of the chat for the entire day has been about food. How many rounds of sandwiches each kid brought, how many different fillings, any egg? Yeuch. There were always a few who had to go the extra mile with different types of bread too. Then there were all the chocolate bars and crisps and drinks. If everyone on the planet died and all the organic life was poisoned while this one bus of ten year old school kids survived, the human race would have been adequately provisioned for a few years. Nick has nothing much but lots of money. When your dad dies you get paid by all the adults around you, as if they are hiring your grief as a vehicle for their own lives, paying him to feel bad, Nick feels guilty to be profiting even though he hasn't asked for it.

And in this small town he sees his dad. Not dead at all; one instant of joy but Nick knows then he has, finally, gone mad. He's mad and imagining things, other boys have been bullying along these lines, how he would become or already was, off his head with grief.

Still he stalks this man and follows him from the toilets to the restaurant of the rest stop and the dad sits down with a woman and a kid and then the dad puts mustard and mayonnaise on the side of his plate and mixes them together and proceeds to dip his chips into this relish. Nick has only ever seen his dad do that, legacy of summers working on the continent. Dad would twirl his adorned chip in the air with a flair Mum called French and set her laughing with a cod accent; sunshine and happiness and mustard and mayonnaise wrapped the memory.

Nick can't even shout he is so overcome. He creeps up behind the table, feeling his legs begin to tremble and turn to jelly, afraid he is going to piss himself as his whole body flashes boiling hot to shivery cold. He whispers, Dad, trying his very best to get it out. To project the most important word ever across the empty air. It stays a whisper and he is unnoticed by this happy family. Smiling mother with pretty eyes and small toddler child in pink and his dad in the middle of this other family. The wrong family.

He is too caught up in the emotional earthquake to be aware of any disturbance away from this hurricane centre. In the distance the class is being called to order, called to the bus, reminded to go to the toilets whether they needed to or not, all the paraphernalia of transport and responsibility. The hushed loudness of corralling kids, especially happy kids. And as he edged towards his dream the roll is being called, there in the restaurant, just a few sets of tables away from all the lucky punters who weren't teachers. And while he whispers his hope into the busyness of everyone else's transience, Miss Caffrey is repeating 'Nick Ganley' and waiting less and less time between each repetition so that even if his ears had still been open to that universe there would have been no time for him to answer. An endless litany of Ganley, Nick, Ganley, Nick, Ganley, Nick, Ganley building to a frustrated squawk because Miss Caffrey always knew they'd lose one but she hopes that the repetition will be a prayer to hold the irritation and extra work of tracking down the selfish tick at bay. And, because she is kind at heart, really wishing that it wasn't this particular hurt boy lost.

So, of course, the baying hounds of class 4C joined in, Niiiiiiick Gaaaaaaanley, Niiiiiiiiick Gaaaaaaaanley. Until everyone in the food court was looking across at the school group. The teachers were hot and bothered. Confused between hushing this helpful riot in front of them and leaving it play out in the hopes that Nick bloody Ganley would appear from where ever he'd slipped off to. Only one table didn't respond, the lady smiled over at the high spirits but the daughter was too busy investigating her brownie for hidden marshmallows. The dad seemed to be frozen, not just still but stiller even then the support pillars of the restaurant, out of phase with everyone else's reality. With extreme reluctance his head began to turn towards the noise and anyone looking could see that his neck tendons were winning a vicious fight to the death with his spine by achieving any movement at all.

Yet even as he forced his eyes to the left, a victorious bay of success sounded and half the hyper class streamed across the food court. In their wake, and converging from all sides now, came officials who knew that patrons' tolerant grins for youthful high spirits were transient at best. In full cry the boys shouted, 'There he is, over there, look, behind that table.'

Even as his eyes registered the tide of junior humanity bearing down on him, the dad's ears interpreted the whistling sounds of the kids triumph. Behind him, behind him, BEHIND him. Like being in a twilight zone pantomime. Again his neck independently took charge and whipped his head to the right. So he is looking straight at Nick and Nick is looking straight at him and the mum

49

and the daughter are smiling in the midst of the hullaballoo and Miss Caffrey reaches her truant charge and puts her hand irrevocably on his stiff shoulder. She knows there are civilians within easy hearing distance and spares only a moment to wish corporal punishment is still acceptable before swinging around to apologise to the disturbed family nearby. And then the tact that had been a defining force in Caroline Caffeys' marriage and divorce swung to the forefront as her smile of apology died and with simple astonishment she says,

'Why, Dominic Ganley, fancy meeting you here, I thought you were dead!'

Emer Barrett

Zombie Stars

Who do you think you are?
I could be a shining star
light torpedoing from space
darkness pierced by history
because experts say now
that the star we see is dead
the star that might be me.

I could be the ocean
the sickly edge
swirling endlessly; bracketing the huge
rubbish pile in the Pacific
that would be terrific.

Or I could be a volcano
quietly resting, gracious and lofty
but inside the melting earth
cascades and bubbles
you think you have troubles?

Or I could be a bee
one of many, lost in a crowd
doomed to die in self defence
but living fully a life of no pretence
born to be the best bee I can be
maybe that most suits me.

Peter Carton recently re-
joined Gorey Writers after
a break of 8 years. He
enjoys writing plays,
poems and short stories.

Black and Tans

One day my father told me of an event that took
place in the Kilkenny town of Greag na Managh.

It was a wet day and he and four other rebels
were being held on a pathway along the Barrow
River. They were being guarded by a single
member of the Tans who looked as miserable as
his prisoners. Compared to his comrades, there
was something different about him.

The rain got worse and my father wondered
how long it would be before they would be taken
to jail. Certainly, it would be more comfortable
than standing in the torrential rain. Still, they all
waited – getting more and more miserable. After
a while the Tan walked up to my father and said,
'Listen mate, next time I march by, the two of
you hit me a wallop and knock me out. Otherwise
you'll all be finished off when the rain is over.'

My father and Jimmy waited for him to return
and when Jimmy hit him he dropped like a tree
and the rebels took off and lived to tell the tale.

Peter Carton

A Children's Home - Aged Three

The bars were strong
too high to climb,
he stood there waiting,
alone.

No one to hold him,
to see his tears
as he stood there waiting,
alone.

The light got dimmer
then it was dark
and he stood there waiting,
alone.

A lamp turned on,
some voices sounded
so he lay down waiting,
alone.

Her head bent over,
she stroked his head
then left him waiting,
alone.

Maura Condren enjoys the creative and social aspect of the Gorey Writers. She finds the group encourages all levels of writing.

Comfort

Well groomed from hours of attention
     stretched out on my lap
front toe to back leg extended
     a contented covering of fur
ginger and snow-white perfection
     the warmth better than any rug
comfort and warmth for both of us.

The Old House

Most people can remember two generations, their parents and their grand-parents. It's as if nobody existed before that, and we all know that there are hundreds and thousands of generations stretching back into prehistory. I have been told that ten generations of my family lived in this house but I have no way of knowing if this is true.

I remember the old house well. It stood at one side of a square with two other sides taken up with outhouses, one was a cowshed and the other was a hayshed. The hayshed contained a little cubicle which housed a commode that I never used as I preferred doing 'my business' in a field, as I think everyone else did.

Every couple of years the buildings were lime washed and were sparkling white. A red climbing rosebush hung over one corner. At this corner of the square, a large barrel stood in the corner. A metal grid lay flat on top of the barrel. This barrel was to collect rain water, and the grid stopped anything large dropping into the barrel. There was no running water in the house but a little spring surfaced in the river field from which we would collect a bucket of water fit for drinking. The collected rain water was used for washing. It wouldn't pass current living standards.

I have great memories of this house and I feel sad that the old way of living is gone. I don't want to romanticise it, as they didn't have much in the way of goods or money, but maybe we lost something important on the way. They didn't need to worry about hoarding stuff because the stuff wasn't there.

The lay-out of the house was traditional in rural Ireland. There were three rooms: the parlour, the kitchen and a bedroom. The attic was used for the children to sleep in. The entrance door brought you into the middle room which was the kitchen and the most important room in the house. On entering there was a wall immediately in front of you, which had a small window. This wall was a wind breaker for the person sitting on the inside who could peep out through the window to see who had entered the house. There was a raised platform on which an open fire was always lighting. The chimney was so wide that you could stand at the fire and look up the chimney and see the sky. This was when I knew that Santa Claus could fit down this chimney. Santa Claus had to be a shape shifter to come down the regular town chimney.

Over the fire was a horizontal pole from which hung perpendicular bars with holes at intervals from which hooks were suspended and pots hung from. These hooks could be moved up or down these bars to either raise or lower the cooking utensil according to the heat required for cooking. Bread could be baked by burying a covered pan into the fire.

The best bit of technology attached to the working of this fire is 'the fanners'. The platform on which the fire was built had a hollow chamber through which air could be funnelled by turning the wheel of 'the fanners'. The stronger and quicker a person turned the wheel the fiercer the fire burnt. There was a shelf near the chimney which acted as their hot press for airing clothes. I thought the clothes always looked dull but maybe not dirty. There was nothing to protect these clothes from the smoke. In fact the smoke from the fire was probably an unhealthy atmosphere to live in, although it didn't stop generations living into old age.

The food cooked seemed to be mainly boiled cabbage, potatoes and some meat. There was no fridge. A metal press completely covered with pierced holes rested on a stone bench outside the house. Butter, jam, milk and sugar was stored here in the fresh air and protected from animals eating it. The kitchen had a radio which was their only entertainment. Later, there was a fridge and a TV.

In photographs, I saw a wooden stairs which led to the attic where the children would have slept. This stairs was removed, and was gone by the time we arrived, but we were the youngest strand of the family and nobody had slept up those stairs for years. Needless to say, there was no bin collection because there was no rubbish. There was no packaging as everything was bought uncovered and everything was eaten.

In the end, the old people died and the fires weren't lit anymore. It was then discovered that water was bubbling up from the ground between the slabs of stone on the kitchen floor. There were no foundations. While the house was lived in the house was living, but when the people died, the house died. There are only ghosts there now and I feel sad. In a hundred years' time nobody will remember me either. We are only passing through.

Krystyna Wiatrowska is a Polish
poet, writer, performer and sculptor.
She has published four books and has
won several poetry awards. Her poems
are translated by Marek Kaźmierski.

a lullaby of liquid nitrogen for you

a homeless dog is howling at me,
though everyone is dead in their beds,
all alone with themselves, evenly
and with distance absorbing shadows
into lungs, expelling dusk in which the dog
                              chokes at the final note.
This down to the cold with greater energy
i turn into a myth about the one and
only light to which one can howl. i know
i am sticking in someone else's throat,
someone freezing all alone with themselves,
pulling onto their back skin
with a negligible degree of warmth. howl to me
- since this gives you relief,
             since this there is no one else here.

Krystyna Wiatrowska

for a boy, returning from a tour of duty
in Afghanistan

writing about the thousandth change of state
and upheavals,
i suspect subcutaneous formations will retreat,
is this how you terrorise, psyche? If i return,
it is only in other fragments, incomplete,
remembering landfills of illusions
about communion, while existence
is entertainment with distracting digressions,
there is within it the fatalism of fission
and the constructor's plan of connections.
i'm just sat here, while
knowledge of this seeks excitement.
if you were to gather much, discard nothing,
escape like hissing air beyond the fields
of illusion! let's start with facts:

to disentangle language means to
stare backwards, dearie, die in the attempt
to simplify and be born in the first light beam:
light touches,
warms and illuminates nothing
in place,
where terrorised i sit and avoid the self.

i feel better in this haven of abstracts than
in relativistic digressions, slowly coming to accept
fragments of limbs and memories of sands, rocks
and the launch which returned my psyche to me.
small losses are missions.

Gerry Walsh is a recent member of Gorey Writers. He enjoys writing prose and plays and the support and camaraderie of the group.

The River
An Acrostic Poem

The
Heat in this glade
Energises.

Rivulets within the river
I find relaxing as they break away
V-shaped
Eddies all
Rejoin and are swept along.

Zoe Buckley has a degree in Creative Writing from Warwick University. She has written two novels and also enjoys writing poetry.

Blessed

One day you and me
we'll meet each other and you will see
we'll laugh at each other's jokes
cry at each other's tales
we'll sit on the bandstand
and talk of our sails
to faraway lands
and weird cultures
one day you and me will see
what the future holds,
what it will be.

2am

Eyes flicker like a shutter
changing nothing of what I see
the light switch scuttles away
        beneath my fingers
over the estate
children sit on walls and
        smoke cigarettes
and a car alarm sings its plea
my dream bothers me
I haven't seen him in years
– and anyway –
I'm over him
he's over me
a moth flutters
I'm lost to sleep
I'm free.

Zoe Buckley

Ape Man

Get inside my mind
the ancient mind that told stories
where the cave roof once opened to the sky
stumble in, bed down and feel grief
for ancestors long gone
search through the silt
for the remains of animals
find the Venus figurine, broken
among bones split open
for the marrow inside.

See the markings on the rocks
where complex worlds converge
in story and mythology –
they haunt without speaking.

During the night-long dances
there were visions in the darkness
(travelling underground,
shooting through a tunnel
dying and coming to life
and flying . . . feeling weightless
- floating above everyone -).

See inscribed on the wall
depictions of early experience
belief is passed on through
grids, tunnels, spirals, funnels

spray the pigment as we did
the rock face will suggest the vision
- it is a membrane between two realms
that share the need to make sense
       of what the brain makes us feel not think.

Courtown Woods

Back in the 50s going to Courtown
fishing for crocodiles
throwing a stick.
When I imagine a tree
true happiness can be attained
it brought back happy memories.
We are dragons, we are real
found a place, so good to be here
all enriched by each other's participation
each supporting each other in a fresh bed.
Today was the worst day ever,
caught a silver trout
there is something good in everyday
two roads diverge in yellow wood
in leaves no step had trodden,
black clears the mind.

*Group Poem written in Courtown Woods, Sunday
16th August 2015: Declan, Catherine, Jacinta,
Chris, Maura, Nora, Yvonne, Mattie, Carol, Simon,
Joyce, Jazz, Anne, Grace and Bernie*